# Herbert Hedgehog in Hogspital Rescue

## How to Help our Hedgehogs

Written and Illustrated

by

R Butler

# DEDICATION

# &

# ACKNOWLEDGMENTS

For all my family and friends and hedgehog lovers, everywhere.

Thank you to Angie Marshall, for your inspiration – and the hedgehog stories!

Copyright © 2017 R Butler

All rights reserved.

Photocopy activity pages 17 - 21 only.

ISBN-10: 1979729808

ISBN-13: 978-1979729802

HELP OUR HEDGEHOGS

SMALL STEPS WE CAN ALL TAKE TOGETHER TO HELP SAVE OUR SPIKY LITTLE FRIENDS.

# Herbert the Rescue Hedgehog

This is Herbert the hedgehog. He is our hero hedgehog. Can you help him rescue his hedgehog friends today?

Follow Herbert on his travels. He will teach you lots of good ideas about how to help hedgehogs. Today's rescue mission! Go!

# Hedgehog Highway

Build a hedgehog highway. Link your garden by making a small hole in your fence about 13cm square.

## Go Wild

Leave a small corner of your garden wild; build a log pile for more nesting and feeding opportunities.

## Food and Water

Put out meaty cat or dog food, mealworms and a dish of water. You could make a feeding station. Put bowls of food under cover near your hog house. See page 17.

## Perilous Ponds

Heidi hedgehog has slipped in the perilous pond! She needs an escape ramp to climb out. Time to rescue!

A simple ramp in a steep sided pond will help Heidi climb out and avoid drowning.

## Killer Chemicals

Harry hedgehog has eaten too many slugs. Poisonous slugs! Slug pellets are toxic to hedgehogs and other animals and birds. Time to rescue! Avoid using toxic slug pellets they are harmful to many creatures.

# Lethal Litter

Hatty hedgehog is in a tangle. She is trapped in lethal litter. Time to rescue!

## Safe Strimming and Monster Mowers!

Holly hedgehog was enjoying the long luscious grass. Oh look! Oh no! Watch out for monster mowers! Time to rescue!

## Bonfires!

Hazel hedgehog loves to sleep during the day. No Hazel! Not the bonfire, don't sleep there! Find another cosy pile of sticks and leaves. Time to rescue!

## Daytime Rescue

Hugo hedgehog is out and about during the day. Hedgehogs are nocturnal. They are night creatures that sleep during the day. Hugo needs to go to bed! Time to rescue!

## Hibernation

Hedgehogs eat a variety of bugs and beasties (slugs, beetles, caterpillars, snails…) When the weather turns colder and food is harder to find, they slow down to save energy and build a nest to over-winter in.

## How to Rescue

As hedgehogs are nocturnal, any seen during the day are in trouble even if they appear lively. By the end of October or when bad weather is expected, any underweight hedgehogs (less than 450g) may need rescuing. Pick the hedgehog up with a towel, place it in a high-sided box lined with newspaper, then seek advice from your local animal rescue centre.

# How to make a Hog House

You will need:
+ A medium sized box, wood or plastic
+ Some adult help cutting
+ Leaves and twigs

1. Cut two air vents and an entrance (approx. 13cm).

2. Lay leaves and twigs inside.

3. Put the box under a hedge with the entrance facing SOUTH.

SOUTH

# Hedgehog Wordsearch

```
M S L U G S L A C I M E H C G
R A U T U M N O S A E S G A H
N H K P A S P I K Y A N P T E
U E N P P E Z F T G L K Z E D
B N N B L O G S W D W B P R G
E E G L A N R U T C O N Y P E
U T E A N O I T A N R E B I H
C T B T T I L P F O M D X L O
S I H I L S L I A N S R E L G
E N P P B E R W T L E A H A C
R G X S H E S D R T V G G R P
G I F G H I O L N E E V A S G
M L P O N D S I S K T R L Y B
R I J H O T W W D P M A T F J
W Z O J Y D U N T F D K W S U
```

AUTUMN
CATERPILLARS
GARDEN
HIBERNATION
LITTER
NETTING
PONDS
SEASON
SPIKY
WILD

BEETLES
CHEMICALS
HEDGEHOG
HOGSPITAL
LOGS
NOCTURNAL
RESCUE
SLUGS
SUPPORT
WINTER

BONFIRE
FOOD
HELP
LEAVES
MEALWORMS
PELLETS
SAVE
SNAILS
WATER

18

# COLOURING PAGE

# Quick Quiz!

1. What is a hedgehog highway?

2. How can a log pile help hedgehogs?

3. List the things that hedgehogs like to eat.

4. What can be added to a pond to help hedgehogs?

5. Why is litter described as lethal?

6. What does nocturnal mean?

7. What can you do in your garden to help hedgehogs?

8. Draw your own hedgehog pictures and write a rescue story about them.

# Hiding Hogs! How many can you find?

## Need more advice?

Contact your local animal rescue centre.

Now you know all about how to help hedgehogs.

Herbert hedgehog thanks you for caring.

There's always time to rescue!

Space for your Hedgehog notes and drawings!

Printed in Great Britain
by Amazon